THE ROBOT AND REBECCA AND THE MISSING OWSER

by Jane Yolen

Text illustrations by Lady McCrady

Alfred A. Knopf ■ New York

2 4 6 8 10 9 7 5 3 1

Library of Congress Cataloging in Publication Data
Yolen, Jane. The robot and Rebecca
and the missing owser. (Capers)
Summary: Rebecca and her mechanical companion investigate
the mysterious disappearance of two rare, dog-like animals
known as owsers.
[1. Science fiction   2. Mystery and detective
stories. 3. Robots—Fiction] I. Title II. Series.
PZ7.Y78Rn 1981   [Fic]   81-4870
ISBN 0-394-84832-2 pbk.   AACR2
ISBN 0-394-94832-7 (lib. bdg.)

This one is for
LIANE
whose charm
is no mystery at all

Contents

85-122

The Robot and Rebecca
and the Missing Owser

1

Looking for a Crime

It was a nice day. Rebecca Jasons could tell by reading the sun-o-meters on the street corners. Since buildings in Bosyork were many stories high, the sun did not shine directly on any of the apartment-city streets very often. So the meters had to flash out the weather news.

"Tuesday, July 13, 2121," Rebecca read out loud. "A.M. 11:15. 29 degrees C. Sun bright and shining." She looked up. Rebecca could see the tall buildings with their thousands of windows like eyes. But she couldn't see any sunshine. Still, the meters said it was bright and shining, and it certainly wasn't raining.

Rebecca turned to her robot, Watson II, and said, "That means it's a nice day."

Watson nodded his silver head but did not answer.

"And maybe it's a nice day—for a crime," Rebecca said hopefully. She wanted to be a detective when she grew up, but she wanted to practice now. She had programmed Watson II to be her detective-helper. "Do you think we might find one?" she asked him.

"Our chances are 1 in 17,568,210," said Watson. His lights flashed across his chest panel as he spoke.

"HELP!" came a sudden cry from several streets away. "Help! Stop thief!"

"Make that 1 in 3," Watson said. His head case cracked open. A small antenna came up and turned toward the sound.

"Why 1 in 3?" asked Rebecca. She stood on her toes trying to see who was screaming. The streets were unusually empty. All she saw were three snakemen from the planet Hisssssss crawling across the road. And a school group of Flitters were practicing takeoffs in an empty lot.

"HELP!" the cry came again.

"I calculate 1 in 3," said Watson, "because that cry is coming from three blocks away. The chances are that it will be answered by the police robots before we get there."

"Then we'd better get moving," said Rebecca. "I'll follow you."

Watson began to roll toward the sound, the tiny wheels on the bottoms of his metal feet whirring pleasantly. The air was still, and sounds carried well. Rebecca could hear the clankings of the apartment-city at work. She loved them all: the silly chatter of the speakers, the whooshing of water along the flush lanes, the clicks of computer keys. It was the sound of the apartment-city at work, and the apartment-city never rested. Rebecca smiled as she ran past Watson, her three braids bouncing against her neck. Watson trailed behind.

"They sure didn't build you for speed," Rebecca said, looking over her shoulder. Watson was silent and kept rolling.

They crossed two more streets and rounded the corner. And there they found a woman crying. Three police robots stood near. Two were holding her hands and making soothing noises. One was taking notes.

"Just give us the facts, lady," said the copbot with the note pad. "Just the facts."

The woman's purse lay at her feet. Her hat was covered with plastic cherries as big as oranges, and it was tilted at a crazy angle on her head.

"It's my owser," she said. "My brand-

new, prize-winning owser. It's gone." She began to cry once more.

"Just the facts, lady," the copbot repeated in a monotone. "Just the facts, lady. Just the facts, lady."

Rebecca walked up to the copbot and pounded it on the back.

The copbot coughed twice and added, "What is your name, lady? And your room number, lady?"

Rebecca shook her head and turned to Watson. "There is so little crime in Bosyork. Not like some of the newer apartment-cities. Nobody bothers to keep the copbots in good working order. They're always getting stuck."

"Since there are so few crimes," Watson put in, "it is not logical to waste human-power cleaning them."

"I'm glad it's not logical," said Rebecca happily. "Because if the copbots don't work properly, then you and I will have to solve the few crimes that do happen. And when we're older, we'll be detectives on the stars—Sherlock Holmes in space." She began to grin broadly. And behind her glasses her eyes shone. "You know," she said to Watson, "it really *is* a nice day." She could almost feel the sun.

2

What's an Owser?

The smile on Rebecca's face suddenly vanished. She bit her lip. Then she leaned over and whispered to Watson, "What's an owser?"

Watson's bank of lights sputtered red, green, and yellow. "An owser is—" he began. Then he stopped.

Rebecca glared at him. "Well? I'm counting on you, you know. We're a team, only you have to do your part."

Watson was silent.

Rebecca nudged him again. "Well?"

"I have no information on owsers," Watson whispered back. Then he added, as if not quite believing it himself, "There is nothing in my memory banks about them."

"Watson!" Rebecca said. "You *have* to know. You *have* to help. That's what you're here for."

"That is logical," said Watson. His voice sounded sad. "But I do not have an answer for you."

Just then one of the copbots spoke. "And what is an owser, lady?" Its voice was low, and it was trying to sound concerned.

"An owser," she said, tears starting up in her eyes again, "an owser is a dear little cutesy-pie. I just loved mine to pieces. It was paper-trained and ate from my own plate and slept at the foot of my bed."

The copbot was busy writing down everything the woman said. But Watson shook his head.

"That answer is illogical," he said loudly.

"Pies are not cute. There are soyberry pies or bran pies. If you loved a pie to pieces, it would be messy, not stolen. Pies do not eat or sleep, and you do not leave them at the foot of your bed. That is illogical. It does not compute."

"Oh quiet," snapped Rebecca. "Of course it's illogical. But I know just what she means."

"Of course you do," said the woman, patting Rebecca's hand. "After all, *you* are human—not a bot. They can only repeat what a human has told them to say." She handed Rebecca a card with her name and address on it. "Call me if you find my dear little owser. I'll see that you get a rich reward." Then she took a whistle from her pocketbook and blew on it.

At the signal, a big black autocycle drove around the corner and stopped by them. The door opened, and a scoop came out. It picked the woman up and placed her gently in the passenger seat. As she straightened

her hat once again, the autocycle took off on a cushion of air.

"Just the facts," the copbot called after her.

Rebecca slammed the copbot on the back and walked off. "Come on, Watson," she said over her shoulder. "We have some detecting to do. At the library."

"That is not called detecting," said Watson. "That is called homework." But he followed her down the street.

3

The Book Worm

At the door of the library, Rebecca held her palm up to the lock. The scanner read her palm print. Then it sent the information to its central computer thirty-seven stories below. Since she had no overdue books, tapes, or discs, the door opened. Rebecca stepped inside, and Watson followed.

The loudspeakers warned them:

Pay attention to the date,
Do not bring your books back late.

The song was repeated to each human and each alien who came through the door.

"*You* may not know what an owser is," Rebecca said to Watson, "but Central Library will. Central Library knows *everything*."

"It is impossible to know *everything*," Watson said. His face plate began to glow a pale green color.

"Why Watson," said Rebecca, as they came into the reference room. "I think you're jealous."

"That is illogical," said Watson. "Jealousy is a feeling. A robot has no feelings."

"Hmmmmmm," was all Rebecca replied.

The encyclopedias took up two entire walls. Rebecca looked under *O,* for *owser.* Nothing.

She looked under *ouser* and *owcer.* Nothing.

She looked under *H* for *howser,* under *A* for *auser,* and even under *E* for *eouser,* since Watson suggested it.

-15-

"Nothing," she said. "*N* for *nothing*."
The loudspeakers sounded right away:

Silence in the hallway,
Silence in the stacks,
Silence is the only way
To take in all the facts.

Watson made a rude noise. Rebecca laughed.

"But we still don't know what an owser is," she said. She sat down and put her chin in her hands. "And Central Library is no help."

Watson's lights played merrily across his chest, and he let out a noise that sounded a great deal like Rebecca's *hmmmmmm*.

"An owssssssser? You want to know what an owssssssser isssssss?" came a hissing voice from behind a stack of books.

Rebecca looked over the books by standing on her tiptoes. A snakeman in a green stocking cap peeked up at her. His tongue darted in and out. His eyes were like emeralds.

"Yes, yes we do," said Rebecca. "But how can you know when the encyclopedias do not?"

"Becausssssssse," said the snakeman, smiling at her, "I am an old book worm. One of the lasssssssst on my planet, Hissssssss. We've mosssssssstly been replaced by tele-wormsssssss. Jussssssst a minute and I'll think of the ansssssssswer."

He put on a pair of glasses, closed his eyes, and curled into a coil. The rattles on his tail shook, and he began to hiss like a

teapot gone mad. Then suddenly his eyes popped open.

"Got it!" he said.

Rebecca frowned. "How could you get it?"

"How? Becaussssssse I have total re-coil," said the snakeman.

"You mean total re*call*," said Watson.

"That'sssssss what I sssssssaid," he answered. "Everything I have ever read—and I read all the time—comessssssss back to me when I am curled up like thisssssss."

"Then, what *is* an owser?" asked Rebecca, being very careful not to hiss back at him. It was quite catching, and she didn't want to hurt his feelings.

"An owsssssssser," hissed the book worm, rising and stretching, "isssssss a ssssssssmall, three-legged, long-haired empath from the K-9 galaxy. And now, if you don't mind, I musssssssst go to the little sssssssssnake's room. Recoiling issssssss rough on me." He took off his glasses, patted his cap with his tail, and crawled out the door.

"What did he mean by all that?" asked Rebecca. She looked more puzzled than before. "I didn't understand a word of it."

"Of course not. You're only human after all," said Watson. If a robot could look smug, he did. "But everything he said was logical. Quite logical. And quite easy to compute." He rolled out the door.

Rebecca jumped up after him. "You big tin can!" she shouted. "Don't run off. Tell me what he said."

The loudspeakers started singing the song about silence, but neither Rebecca nor Watson paid any attention.

4

Another Crime

"Tell me, tell me," Rebecca begged when she caught up with Watson. She pushed his question button three times hard. Watson began explaining. "The K-9 galaxy is a place where all the life came from dogs."

"So an owser would be a doggy kind of creature," said Rebecca.

"Logical," Watson answered.

"Okay, I understand that much now. But what is an empath?" Rebecca folded her arms and waited for Watson's answer. She loved listening to him explain things.

He was more than just a robot to her. He was more than just a present she had gotten for her ninth birthday. He was her friend.

"An empath," said Watson, "is a being that understands and feels all the things its closest friends feel."

Rebecca sat down on the curb and put her hands on her knees. The robot sat next to her, his joints squeaking.

"You mean," Rebecca said, lifting her legs for a minute to let the lane flush water along the road, "like a best friend?"

"No, even closer. An empath can *only* feel what you feel, and make you feel it even more," said Watson.

"So an empath would be happy because I was happy—"

"Or sad because you were sad," finished Watson. "And would make you feel it even more." Since he had not been told to do so, he did not lift his legs, and the water from the flush lane soaked them.

"Oh, oh," warned Rebecca, "lift up or you'll rust." She opened the small door in Watson's back. He leaned back, legs in the air, over the flush lane. Inside the small door was a can of No-Rustum. She sprayed his ankles and the wheels under his feet. Then she put the can back.

Watson turned himself around with his hands and stood up on the sidewalk. He kicked his feet one at a time to get the oil deep into the joints.

"What does not compute," he said as he kicked, "is that empaths are usually not sold as pets. They are too valuable. They

are used in high government circles and for important meetings. There is a law about how many can be sold and where. Law number 348598265820678830414-240950031-0986524437582669274-9. It is—"

"HELP! HELP!" voices cried suddenly, stirring the air.

Rebecca jumped up. "Another crime," she said happily. "Two in one day. That must be a record these days." She began to run toward the sound.

"Actually," Watson put in, "there were two crimes on February 11, 2119, in San Frangeles. And two more on May 21, 2107, in Chiappolis. And here in Bosyork, on April 30—"

"Oh, come on," shouted Rebecca.

The robot started rolling after her. But since she had not ordered him to stop talking about crimes, his voice went on and on and on as he rolled.

Across the street and down a block, in front of a Grow-cery store, were two crying children. The boy, who was about seven, had bright blue tears running down his face. The girl, who seemed younger, was crying orange.

Rebecca ran across the run lane. Watson followed carefully in the roll lane. Above them, in the fly lane, the school of Flitters flew back for recess.

There were no copbots in sight. Rebecca ran up to the two crying children and held out her arms. The little girl ran right into Rebecca's coveralls. She left a bright orange spot. The boy just rubbed a blue blot across his cheeks. Rebecca knew right away that they were visitors from the Rainbow galaxy.

"There, there, kids," said Rebecca. "What's wrong?"

The little girl went on crying, but the boy spoke up.

"It's our owser," he said. "It's been owse-napped."

5

Just the Facts

The little girl looked up, a bright orange tear hanging from the corner of her eye. "He was our pet. We had just gotten him from our daddy. And now the owser's gone."

Both children began sobbing again, the boy louder this time than the girl.

The city speakers sang brightly:

Do not cry and do not sob,
Bot-police are on the job.

It finished with a loud siren. In less than

thirty seconds, two copbots had appeared. They sat the children on their metal laps and patted them with tin hands.

"Just tell us the facts, kids," the copbots said together. "Just the facts."

Rebecca snapped at them angrily. "These kids have already told us the facts." She spoke directly into the copbots hearing holes. "Their owser has been owsenapped."

The children ran out from under the tin hands and back to Rebecca. They both grabbed at her.

"You'll help us find him, won't you?" asked the boy.

"You bet," she said. "My name is Rebecca, and this is Watson," she said. "Solving crimes is our job."

The copbots rolled away, their wheels squeaking terribly.

The Rainbow boy held Rebecca's hand

as he told her his story.

"We were given the owser for our name day," he said.

"What's a name day?" asked Rebecca.

Watson answered for them. "Name days take the place of birthdays in the Rainbow galaxy. Each day has a special name instead of a month and number. When it is your name day, you have a party and get presents."

"And my name is Iri. My sister here is—"

"Iris," the little girl said.

"Our parents work for the government, so they were allowed to buy an owser. They got it at a Pettery," said Iri. "They said the Pettery sold pets from all over the universe, but that an owser was the best of all. We named our owser Ir, so it could share our name day."

"And what did Ir look like?" asked Rebecca.

"Well, he was three-legged, of course," said Iri.

"Of course," said Watson.

"And he looked like a dog," Iris continued. "With doggy ears and a doggy tail."

"And what does that mean?" asked Watson, shaking his silver head.

"You know what a doggy tail is," said Rebecca quickly. "It's what's on the other end of a dog. Do be quiet."

Iris laughed, and Iri went on. "And he had long, pepper-colored hair."

Lights flashed across Watson's chest. "Pepper-colored does not compute. There is no such color."

Rebecca freed her hand from Iris's and patted the little boy on the head. "I think he means it had black spots on white."

"That's right," said Iris. "That's what he means. Pepper-colored." Her tears had stopped, and her eyes were ringed with orange. "And he was as cute as—"

"Pie," said Watson, remembering the woman with the cherry hat.

"Pie isn't cute," said Iris, looking at the robot strangely. "It's soyberry or bran."

"He was as cute as an owser should be," finished Iris. "And he seemed to always know what I wanted or how I felt."

"Me too," said Iri.

"That is logical," said Watson. "An owser is an empath."

"Then what happened?" Rebecca asked.

Iri scratched his head. His fingernails were as blue as his tears. "That's the funny part. We took him for a walk. He seemed to love to go out whenever we wanted to go out. We stopped back at the Pettery to get him some treats. Then we walked to the Kandi store. We both went in to get some lollipops for us. And some lollipups for Ir."

"Because he was a sort of a dog," his sister added. "Only with three legs."

"And we tied him carefully to a fire

-29-

hydrant outside the store. With a double knot," said Iri.

"Only when we came out—" Iris said.

"Let me guess," Rebecca broke in. "The owser was gone."

Watson flashed his lights.

Iri sighed. "That's right," he said.

"But there was something *really* strange," said Iris.

"Stranger than a three-legged dog that disappears into thin air?" asked Watson.

"Stranger than that," said Iri. "Our owser was gone. *And the fire hydrant was gone, too!*"

With that, Iris began to cry again. Great orange tears ran down her cheeks and fell with little *plops*. Soon the sidewalk had so many spots that it looked as if it had a bad case of measles.

Overhead, the city speakers began to shout:

Do not cry and do not sob,
Bot-police are—

"Not needed!" shouted Rebecca, Iri, and Iris up at the speakers. The speakers shut off.

But Watson was still thinking about the disappearing fire hydrant. "That is illogical. That does not compute," he said, shaking his head.

Iri walked over to Watson and poked a finger at his metal chest. "It may not be logical, and it may not compute. But it happened. So it's true."

"And it's a clue!" shouted Rebecca.

"What is true and what is logical are not always the same," said Watson. "There must be some *logical* reason for all this."

Rebecca spoke to the robot. "Logic is your problem," she said. "Solving this crime is mine."

"And mine, too," said Watson.

"So—first things first," said Rebecca. "And the first thing we better do is go to that Pettery." Rebecca looked at the Rainbow kids. "That is, if you know where it is."

"Easy," said Iri and Iris together. "It's not far from here. Come on."

6

The Pettery

The four of them running along the apartment-city street made quite a crowd. Other walkers had to step off into the flush lanes or hug the walls. Still, no one said anything —except for the city-speakers, which sang out along their way:

Right of way is for the fast,
Stay to the right and you'll be passed.
Move to the left and you can go
Past anyone who goes too slow.

"Slow*ly,*" said Rebecca without missing a step. She loved the feel of the city pavement underfoot. The slip-slop sound of her plasti-shoes on the walk. The whirr of Watson's wheels. It made her smile.

Iris and Iri did not smile. Their minds were on their missing pet.

Watson did not smile. Smiling, for a robot, is impossible.

As they turned the corner, Iris pointed down the street. "There it is," she called.

Rebecca looked. In the middle of the block was a Pettery. Its sign showed an earth cow jumping over the many moons of Jupiter.

Rebecca put her hands up and stopped. The others stopped, too. "I think you kids had better stay here for now," she said. "Let us poke around a bit first."

"Ahhh," sighed Iri and Iris. But they put their backs against the wall and waited. Their tears were dry now. Only the orange and blue blots on their cheeks remained. As they stood and watched, they held hands.

Watson and Rebecca crept forward in silence. But Rebecca was too excited to keep still for long.

"You know," she said to Watson, "the only clues we have to go on so far are this Pettery, the missing hydrant, and what we know about owsers."

"That isn't much," grumped Watson.

They moved on and stood in front of the Pettery window. There were many kinds of pets there. A small cage held two tiny red dragons from the McCaffrey galaxy, the kind that ride comfortably on a shoulder pad and breathe out warm smoke to tickle an owner's ear. A white woolly muffle flopped lazily in one corner. The only reason they knew it wasn't a mop was that the muffle sometimes yawned. Hanging from the ceiling was a full string of weedsels, the pet that looked a lot like seaweed. It could live for years in a waterless aquarium. There was also a large jar of slate-colored marbeliters snapping at one another like angry ball bearings.

Rebecca looked at a list of pets pasted onto the window. She read it out loud to Watson:

- Dogs, all kinds, Earth.
- Dragons, small, McCaffrey.
- Eggs, pot luck. We don't know what's in them. Hatch them yourself and take a chance.
- Fowl, earth chickens and small songbirds from Earth, Tew, and many nebulae.
- Marbeliters, from Carver I and II, SALE.
- Muffles, all colors, SPECIAL.
- Serpents, healing snakes and windshield vipers.
- Weedsels, no string alike. Great for small rooms.

- Yo-yos, the pet-on-a-string, from the dark side of the Moon.

"Notice something strange?" Rebecca asked when she finished reading the list.

Watson nodded, his head rattling. "Yes. It does not say anything about owsers. This cannot be the right place."

"That's logical," said Rebecca, "but it might not be true. Remember, they are mostly sold to people in the government. So they wouldn't be on an ordinary list. But the Rainbow kids say they got their owser here."

"Perhaps the kids are wrong," Watson tried.

"Logical. But I don't think so," said Rebecca. "In fact, I'm beginning to smell a rat."

"Rats are not listed either," reminded Watson. "Perhaps it is the muffle you smell."

"It's a rat," said Rebecca. "And don't get mixed up. *To smell a rat* is old slang for *something is not right*. We've done first things first. Now it's time for second things second."

"I'll never understand humans," said Watson.

"But I know someone who does. Someone who also had an owser," said Rebecca, reaching into her pocket. She dug around and came up at last with the card that the woman in the cherry hat had given her. "Here, read this," she said, handing the card to Watson. He held it up to his scanners and read it out loud.

"Mrs. Jay Gregory Van Stebbins, South-West Corridor 753, 754, 755." He put up his metal hands in wonder. "She has *three* rooms. Those South Corridor folk are rich."

"Rich and full of facts. Just the facts, lady, that we need to know," said Rebecca.

7

On the Sub

Running back to the waiting Rainbow kids, Rebecca had no time to enjoy the city sights and sounds. She was trying to remember the best and fastest way to get to the South-West Corridor, 750s.

Watson wheeled behind.

"Come with us," Rebecca called to the kids as she ran past them.

Holding hands, Iris and Iri trotted behind Watson. They all stopped suddenly at the corner because Rebecca was there, standing still, reading the map that was carved into the building wall.

Rebecca put a finger of her right hand high up on the map. "We are here," she said. Then she put a finger of her left hand all the way down near the sidewalk. "And Mrs. Van Stebbins lives there." She could hardly stretch that far.

"How do we get *there* is the question," said Watson.

"We could get an autocab," said Iris and Iri together, though they didn't know who Mrs. Van Stebbins was or why they should go there. All they knew was that they trusted Rebecca.

"How much money do we have?" Rebecca asked suddenly.

The Rainbow kids searched their clothes and came up with seventeen coppers and one Miss America quarter. Rebecca had forty-three coppers, a DisneyMoon dime, and an iron ring from the planet Sizzlegrid that her best friend had given her. Watson carried no money, but he did have a Sub token jammed in his antenna. Rebecca had put it there one day when he'd had trouble with his sound circuits.

"Well, we have enough for the four of us to go by Sub, not autocab," said Rebecca. "Though I'm not sure we'll be able to get back again."

"Maybe we could borrow money from your Mrs. Van Stebbins," said Iri. "She probably has more money than the four of us."

"*She,*" explained Rebecca, "is someone who had an owser. And it was stolen, too."

Iris's orange-ringed eyes got wide. "Then she will surely lend us the money to get back."

"Logical," said Watson. "But only if she is at home."

"Let's try," said Rebecca. "What else can we do?" She started toward the nearest Sub station. The others followed.

Going down the moving stairs, Rebecca was quiet. Pleasant music came from speakers hidden in the pink Sub walls. It made everyone feel sleepy and slow.

Rebecca thought about their three clues. The missing owsers was the first one. Who, she wondered, would want an empath? The answer to that was simple. Anyone.

The second clue was the Pettery. It had not listed owsers. Was that important? Rebecca did not know. Yet.

The third clue was the hydrant. Something told her that was the most important clue of all. But she did not know why. Perhaps someone was stealing hydrants, and the owser just happened to be tied to it. Now *that* made some kind of sense. Stealing hydrants was much harder than stealing owsers. Therefore, it must be the hydrant. She was just thinking about this when Watson's voice broke into her thoughts.

"It would be more logical to vid-phone Mrs. Van Stebbins first," he said.

"If we use our coppers to phone, we

won't have enough left to go there,"
Rebecca explained.

The Sub finally arrived. They pushed
their way on. It was already crowded.
Some passengers were human, but most
were not.

Rebecca stood next to a huge Efflerump
who took up a third of the Sub car.

Iris and Iri were separated by three
Canterloopers. Canterloopers looked like

melons whose vines were all tangled. They smelled like vinegar. And whenever they spoke, they made burping noises. Pretty soon Iris and Iri were burping, too. Being near a group of Canterloopers made any human feel drunk. It was called "being looped."

Watson stood in the corner next to two bots. One was a sweeper, and one was an office worker.

The Sub speakers broke into the soft music at each stop. They sang out the stations with a warning:

Is this the place you want to go?
Use the door and don't be slow.
South-South 640s.

It was a long time before they reached the South-West 750s.

When the speakers told them their station was next, Rebecca called to the others, "This is it. Let's go."

They ran out of the car, and Rebecca found the exit sign. "Let's hope Mrs. Jay Gregory Van Stebbins is home," she said. "It's a long walk back."

"That's the first logical thing you've said all day," said Watson.

Moving stairs took them to the street.

8

A Very Unusual House

Rebecca had never been on one of the rich streets before. The sidewalks were a lot wider. Every now and then, sunlight was able to drift down. The only other time Rebecca had felt sun on her had been on a trip to San Frangeles. Her family had taken a turn standing on the shore. She wasn't sure she liked it all that much. It had made her skin tingle.

There were thin trees planted in blocks of dirt, one to a street. They had guard rails around to protect them. Rebecca ran her hand along the rail. The rail shouted at her:

A friendly warning to the wise,
Don't use fingers, just use eyes.

Rebecca stuck out her tongue and went on down the block. The others followed close behind.

Reaching into her pocket again, Rebecca pulled out the card and read Mrs. Van Stebbins's address once more. Then she checked the street sign. "Around the corner," she said.

Iris and Iri were holding hands. Rebecca reached out and touched Watson's shoulder. "We've never been this far from home by ourselves," she whispered to him.

"Are you afraid, Rebecca?" he asked quietly.

She smiled at him and patted his shoulder. "Me? Afraid? Of course not."

He patted her back clumsily.

Rebecca walked ahead and turned the corner. "Look," she said softly. "Two trees. With leaves."

"She must *really* be rich," said Iri.

Rebecca nodded and turned in at the door marked 750. There was a large robot standing guard. It was wearing a dark blue metal jacket with brass buttons on the front and a dark blue plastic tie.

"A butler robot," whispered Watson to Rebecca. "It is called a but-bot."

"Whom do you wish to see?" asked the but-bot. His voice had just a trace of a British accent.

"Mrs. Jay Gregory Van Stebbins, please," said Rebecca in her most polite voice.

"And whom shall I say is calling?" asked the but-bot, pushing several of his brass buttons.

"Tell her the girl she met today. Tell her it's about her owser."

The but-bot looked down and spoke into his tie. It was a microphone in disguise. "There is a girl to see Mrs. Van Stebbins. About an owser."

Three of the brass buttons lit up. "She will see you," said the but-bot. "Take the elevator to the top floor." He pointed the way.

The elevator doors opened silently, and the four got in.

"Floor, please?" asked a speaker.

"Top," said Watson.

They rode up in silence to the seventy-ninth floor. When they got out, the speaker sang out a good-bye to them.

Mrs. Van Stebbins was waiting at the door to one of her rooms. "I thought," she said a bit confusedly, "that there was a girl. But I see four of you—and one is not even human."

"That's Watson. And Watson is better than human—sometimes," said Rebecca. "And besides, he's my friend."

Mrs. Van Stebbins put her head to one side. "Friend or not," she said, "he'll have to stay off my carpets with his rollers. And who are you?" she asked the Rainbow kids.

Rebecca answered for them. "That's Iri and Iris. And I am Rebecca Jasons."

"Well, my friends call me Ms. Vis," said Mrs. Van Stebbins, shaking hands all around. "It's short for Van Stebbins. And it's easier to remember." She led them into

the room—but first she made them take off
their shoes. Their weight on the carpet
made pillows rise up from the rug to just
the right height for sitting. Ms. Vis and the
children sank down into the soft cushions.

"Now what is this about my owser?
Have you found it?"

Rebecca pulled on one of her braids.
Then she leaned forward. "Not quite yet,

Ms. Vis. But we have some leads. Iris and
Iri had an owser, too. They tied it to a fire
hydrant and went into a store. And when
they returned—"

"Let me guess," said Ms. Vis excitedly.
"It was gone."

"And so was the fire hydrant," said Iris
and Iri together.

"That's what I said," said Ms. Vis.

"No, you said the owser was gone," Rebecca corrected her.

"They were *both* gone," said Ms. Vis. She shook her finger at Rebecca. "You didn't listen."

"You didn't say," Rebecca began. "But that hydrant!" she said, interrupting herself excitedly. Someone *had* been stealing hydrants.

Watson rolled to the edge of the carpet. "We all know why an owser would want a fire hydrant," he said. "Every dog knows the answer to that. But the question we should each be asking ourselves is this: Why would a fire hydrant want an owser?"

Mrs. Van Stebbins jumped up. "What pure logic. You sound like my dear departed husband Jay Gregory. Roll on my rug, Watson. Have a seat. May I call you Watty? You have such . . . such *human* antennae."

"*Watty!*" Rebecca jumped up and ran

over to Watson. The minute she got off the rug, her cushion settled back down in place. "Watty, indeed! We have no time. Watson is right. We *have* been asking the wrong questions. And *I* have been looking at our clues in the wrong way. It's time to ask the right questions—in the right place."

"Where is that?" asked Ms. Vis and the Rainbow kids.

"Yes," said Watson, "where *is* that?"

"At the Pettery," said Rebecca.

85-122

9

Inside the Pettery

They piled into Ms. Vis's autocycle. Iris sat on Iri's lap. Rebecca sat on Watson's lap. Ms. Vis rode up in front with the automatic driver. There was little traffic in the streets besides some tour buses from a water planet in the swim lane. With a little bit of luck, Rebecca thought, they would get to the Pettery before closing time.

"I think we should go in disguise," said Rebecca.

"I don't like costumes," said Ms. Vis, fixing her cherry hat.

"They are not part of my plan," said

Rebecca. "What I mean is that Ms. Vis is going to introduce me in the Pettery as her Very Rich Niece. And you others will stay outside."

"But . . . but . . . but—" Watson sputtered.

"Oh, he does sound like my dear Gregory," said Ms. Vis, turning around and smiling. "Dear Watty."

"Outside," Rebecca said firmly. "You all have to be sure that no one escapes with a hydrant."

"Who do you expect to escape?" droned Watson.

"You never know," Rebecca said. Actually, she had no idea.

The autocycle dropped them off down the block from the Pettery.

"Why, that's the very same Pettery where I bought my owser," said Ms. Vis.

"Logical," Rebecca and Watson said together.

Ms. Vis and Rebecca walked on ahead.

Behind them came Watson and the Rainbow kids. Watson pretended that he was a guide-bot pointing out the sights to Iris and Iri. He was telling them about the buildings when Rebecca and Ms. Vis opened the Pettery door and went in.

The smell of all the pets was very strong. Rebecca turned up her nose. And the sound! There were dogs yapping, marbeliters snapping, serpents hissing, weedsels swishing, muffles snoring, dragons roaring. Only the yo-yos were silent. Rebecca covered her ears and nearly tripped over a gray mop standing by the door.

As the door closed behind them, the store-speaker sang out:

> *Welcome to the Pettery store.*
> *We have what you want—and more.*
> *If we don't have it, we can get*
> *Any kind of strange new pet.*
> *Just ask.*

"I'd like it quiet, please," asked Ms. Vis.

The speakers gave out a strange, high whistle. At that signal, the shop was still.

Suddenly the mop next to Rebecca's arm seemed to fill out. She saw she had made a mistake. It was not a mop at all. It was a man with wild gray hair. He was wearing gray coveralls and gray sneakers and a very false-looking smile. Rebecca wondered how she could ever have thought he was a mop.

"May I help you?" asked the gray man.

"You may indeed," said Ms. Vis before Rebecca could say a word. "My name is Mrs. Jay Gregory Van Stebbins. You may remember I bought an owser from you the other day. It is gone."

"My, my. Gone, you say," said the gray man. "That *is* too bad. They are so very hard to come by. But these things do happen, you know."

Rebecca was about to say, "And they seem to happen too often," but Ms. Vis went on.

"They do. They do indeed. What is this world coming to? Soon it will be as bad as some alien station. But never mind. Money doesn't matter. I had wanted to give the owser to my little niece here. My Very Rich Little Niece. Whose parents are *in the government.*"

"Your Very Rich Little Niece," the gray man repeated. His gray eyes seemed to catch fire. His false smile got even broader.

"Yes," said Rebecca. She was copying Ms. Vis's slow, broad accent. "And money doesn't matter. Do you sell many owsers in a day?" she asked.

The gray man did not answer but smiled his gray smile.

"My Very Rich Little Niece loves to ask questions," said Ms. Vis.

"Yes, I want to be a Very Rich Little Newsfax Person when I grow up," said Rebecca. "Do you sell many owsers in a day?"

"No," the gray man said shortly. "Owsers are not for sale very often. Did you see an owser on our list?"

"No," said Rebecca. "But—"

"But sometimes we can find one for a *special* customer," said the gray man.

"I hope you will think of me as that special customer," said Ms. Vis. "Since I already bought one. I hope you can find *me* another."

-61-

The gray man looked around carefully. He sighed. "I have one in the back room," he said. "But it is the very last one. I shall have to ask double the price of your other owser." Then he smiled again, pulling the smile across his face with the back of his hand. He went into the back room.

Ms. Vis whispered to Rebecca. "How am I doing?"

"Great!" said Rebecca. "But better not say anything about fire hydrants. I'll look around to see if he has any hidden away. You keep him busy." She went over to the cages and pretended to look at the pets. But her eyes were busy searching for fire hydrants.

The gray man returned carrying a fuzzy, three-legged, black-and-white animal. This time the man's smile was real. He was humming.

"That looks just like my own little owser," said Ms. Vis. She checked the animal's ears and paws and tail. Then she checked them again, taking a lot of time.

"Look at this," said Ms. Vis.

The gray man looked.

"This owser has blue eyes, just like mine."

"They all look pretty much alike," said the gray man. He did not notice Rebecca walking all around his store. She peeked in every corner.

At last Ms. Vis took the owser and paid the man. Rebecca came over and took the owser in her arms. Then she and Ms. Vis went out the door.

"Did you see any hydrants?" asked Ms. Vis.

"No hydrants," said Rebecca. She was smiling broadly.

With the owser in her arms, she felt warm and safe and happy. She remembered all her favorite things: soyberry pie, rainy book days, the first time she had seen Watson, playing in her friend Snar's room. She remembered all her favorite sounds and tastes and smells. Bits of her favorite songs floated through her head. She felt that nothing in the world could go wrong as long as she had the owser in her hands. The owser licked her cheek with its little pepper-colored tongue. Rebecca kept smiling. She wondered how anyone could ever let an owser go.

Inside the shop, the gray man pulled the shades down and placed a CLOSED sign on the door. Then he shook his moppy gray head, stood very straight and still, and thought. The smile on his face faded.

10

The Owser

"So *that* is an owser," said Watson. His gears rattled as he sent the information to his tapes. If he ever needed to know what an owser was again, he would be able to find the information in an instant.

"It looks like *our* owser," said Iris and Iri together.

"They all look pretty much alike," Rebecca said, smiling broadly. The owser made her feel happier still.

"Perhaps you can tell us the rest of your plan now," Ms. Vis said. "That was such fun, I am ready for anything."

"Plan? Plan?" Rebecca's voice sounded puzzled, but her face kept smiling.

Watson rolled over to her and took the owser from her arms. He felt nothing but a deep, happy humming.

"Oh, yes, my plan," said Rebecca, looking over at the owser now settled in Watson's silver arms. Rebecca sighed. "I thought I would take the owser for a walk up and down the block and then tie it to a fire hydrant. And you all would watch him while I went into a store."

"And what is the logic of that?" asked Watson.

"Whoever stole the hydrant attached to Ms. Vis's owser and the Rainbow kids' owser might come and steal this hydrant, too. And we can catch him, her, it, or them in the act."

"That's a pretty long shot," said Ms. Vis.

"The odds are 461,098 to 1 that it happens again," Watson entoned.

"But worth a try," said Rebecca.

"Oh yes," said Iri and Iris. They nodded their heads. Iris stuck an orange-nailed thumb into her mouth.

"I will come, too," said Watson. His voice now had a strange hum to it. "Just to keep everybody's head clear." He reversed one of his arms and opened the box in his back. He searched around in the box until he came up with a piece of yellow string. "We can walk the owser with this."

Rebecca took the string and tied it to the owser's neck. Then Watson put the owser down on the sidewalk. The owser hummed at Watson for a moment more, then began to trot in circles on its three legs.

"Let's go," said Rebecca. And holding the owser's leash, she started down the street.

Watson and the Rainbow kids walked past her quickly and waited by an Ice Creamery. They pretended to talk together but were really watching Rebecca and the owser.

Rebecca and Ms. Vis let the owser sniff their legs, sniff the sidewalk, and finally sniff and settle against a fire hydrant. It was a red hydrant with a bright blue cap.

"Well," said Rebecca a little too loudly, "I think I will tie my brand new owser to this red fire hydrant and go inside for some ice cream with my aunt." She wrapped the end of the string around the blue cap. They went into the Ice Creamery.

Watson and the Rainbow kids waited outside, trying to look casual. Watson leaned against the store window and hummed. Iri stuck his hands in his pockets and whistled. Iris took her thumb out of her mouth and ran it across the glass, leaving an orange smear.

The store speakers loudly welcomed Rebecca and Ms. Vis with a ding-dong sound. Rebecca ordered two scoops of pumpkin-pie ice cream and two scoops of sunflower-seed sherbet. She looked out of the window. All she could see was Watson's back. Ms. Vis and Rebecca each took a scoop out to the kids.

The owser still sat happily in front of the hydrant on two of its three legs.

"That didn't work," Rebecca said. "Must be the wrong kind of hydrant. On to the next store."

They went on to a Grow-cery store where they tied the owser to another hydrant. Ms. Vis bought them each a banumber, the newest veg-fruit. It was a cross between a banana and a cucumber. It had yellow and green stripes and mushy yellow seeds.

Rebecca checked the window several times. And when they came out, the owser was still there. It was waiting by the red fire hydrant, scratching its ears with one foot.

They found a red hydrant outside a Liq-uid store. Ms. Vis went inside and bought them some multicolored water.

Then they tied the owser to a red hydrant next to a Sportery, and Ms. Vis got them each rollerball cards of their favorite players.

Each time they went into a store, they found the owser sitting by the hydrant when they came out. One time it had even fallen asleep on the sidewalk. That made them all feel sleepy. Iris yawned, and Ms. Vis rubbed her eyes.

"What's wrong with *these* hydrants?" asked Rebecca angrily. "How come the thief doesn't want any of them?"

No one could answer her.

"Well, my feet hurt," said Ms. Vis.

The others felt the same way. And when the owser started limping as well, they tied it to a hydrant next to a Doctory and went inside to put their feet up on the massager. Even Watson rolled in and got his wheels rubbed.

This time the hydrant was gray with a shaggy gray cap.

When they came out, their feet felt fine. They looked up the street, then down.

"The owser. It's stolen," shouted Ms. Vis. "Kidnapped. Owse-napped. Gone!"

"And so is the hydrant," said Watson. The hum was gone from his voice.

"Now *that's* logical," said Rebecca.

85-122

11

Two Solutions

"Did anyone see anything?" asked Rebecca.

Iris looked up, her eyes full of orange tears. "I looked out the window once," she said. "I think I saw a kind of gray fog."

"Gray fog," repeated Watson. His gears clanked.

"I saw a gray tree over the hydrant when I checked. It shook its leaves," said Iri.

"Gray tree," repeated Watson. His cogs whirred.

"When I looked out, I saw a gray newspaper blowing in the wind," said Ms. Vis.

"It blew in front of the window and blocked my view of the owser."

"Gray newspaper," repeated Watson. His buttons lit up.

"The owser is gone," said Rebecca. "And so is the hydrant. And I forgot to look at all. Some detective I am." She felt ready to cry.

Suddenly Watson started sputtering. "I have it. I have it. The only logical answer." The slot in his stomach opened and started chattering. Paper filled with numbers and letters rolled out. At the bottom of the paper was the word SOLUTION.

Rebecca tore the paper off. "And what *is* the solution?" she asked as she read.

"An invasion from a gray planet," said Watson excitedly. "The gray fog covered their landings. The gray trees were really their soldiers. Or their spaceships. The gray newspaper covered their retreat."

"You call *that* logical?" asked Rebecca.

Iris and Iri shook their heads.

Ms. Vis laughed.

Rebecca continued. "That doesn't make any sense. However, *now* I think I know the answer."

Watson made a huffing sound. He took the paper from Rebecca's hand and threw it into the flush lane. In an instant, a gush of water swept it away down a hole in the street. It would eventually make its way to the great underground dump. There it would be burned for fuel to run the apartment-city.

Rebecca counted on her fingers. "Gray

fog. Gray tree. Gray newspaper. What do they all have in common?''

The Rainbow kids, who learned the names of colors before they learned any other words, answered together. "Gray."

Rebecca nodded. "And there was something else that was the same color," she said.

"The fire hydrant," said Ms. Vis.

Watson mumbled, "I *did* say gray."

"And," Rebecca said slowly, "someone else was gray, too."

"Who?" they all asked together.

"The Pettery man."

Watson looked up, his gears turning so quickly they made sparks. "And he has a gray mop. Is he a witch?"

Rebecca laughed and slapped Watson on the back, making his insides clink and clank together like a sackful of coins. "If he were a witch, he'd need a broom, not a mop. And that was no mop. Not really.

That, my friends, was a mopster."

"A mopster?" asked Iris.

"What's a mopster?" asked Iri.

"A *mobster*. With a *B*," recited Watson. "A mobster is the twentieth-century word for a criminal. A bad guy. A highwayman. A thief."

"And on one planet, Chameleon III, a *mopster* is a thief, too," added Rebecca mysteriously.

"Then we had better go back to the Pettery and confront this mopster," said Ms. Vis.

"Before he sells the owser to someone else," agreed Rebecca, and she started off down the street.

12

The Gray Man

They followed Rebecca around the block. On the way, they bumped into an Efflerump. The enormous alien was so frightened, it took the next rocket for home.

At last Rebecca stopped in front of the Pettery. "Look!" she said, and pointed.

The store was only dimly lit. But they could see the gray man standing near the window. He was holding an owser and smiling.

"Help!" shouted Ms. Vis. "Help! Stop thief."

"Criminal. Highwayman," shouted Iris.

"Mopster," shouted Iri.

Watson opened the Pettery door, and Rebecca ran in just as city speakers chirped brightly:

> *Do not cry and do not sob,*
> *Bot-police are on the job.*

They finished with a loud siren. In less than twenty-two seconds, two copbots appeared.

"In here," called Watson.

The copbots rolled into the store.

Rebecca stood there with her arms around a gray mop. "Here he is," she said. "This is the thief."

"We cannot arrest mops, lady," said one copbot. "There are no laws against mops in the metroplex." It shook its metal head.

"This is not a mop," said Rebecca.

"Begging your pardon, lady," said the other copbot. "But it has a long gray stick.

And a head of fuzzy gray hair. It looks like a mop to me."

"Look more closely," said Rebecca, still holding on to the mop.

The copbots looked more closely. The mop began to change ever so slightly, growing half a dozen gray leaves instead of hair. It wore gray shoes on its roots.

"That's no mop," said Ms. Vis.

"And that's no tree," said the Rainbow kids.

"This is the Pettery owner," said Rebecca. "And I bet he comes from Chameleon III, the planet of people who can change their shapes."

The mop/tree/man began to cry. "I didn't mean to steal the owser back," he said. "I just couldn't bear to let it go. It made me feel so good." As he spoke, the owser jumped out of his arms and sat on the ground at his feet, howling.

"Just the facts, thief. Just the facts,"

said the copbots, holding on to the gray man in case he turned into something else.

"I sold that same owser fifty-seven times," the gray man said. "Each time I would lock up my store, sneak out the back door, and follow the new owner. I would wait on the street corner disguised as—"

"A gray fire hydrant," said Rebecca.

"Logical," entoned Watson.

"How did you know?" asked the man from Chameleon III.

Rebecca shook her head. "If you had worn red pants and dyed your hair red, then you would have been a red fire hydrant. We might never have figured it out. And, if you hadn't been so greedy, wanting to keep the owser and make money, too, you would not have gotten into trouble."

The gray man hung his head.

"You have a right to remain silent," said the copbots to the Pettery owner. They reminded him of all his rights under the

United Planetary Laws. As they took him away, the gray man turned into a gray waterfall that threatened to rust the cop-bots. But they were ready for such tricks and held on tight.

13

The Best Reward

"GIRL NABS MOPSTER" read the head-line in the afternoon paper as it chattered out of the Newsfax slot in Ms. Vis's apartment.

"Here," said Ms. Vis. "Listen to this. We are all mentioned." She read it aloud. *"Rebecca Jasons of 1700/37 NNE Bosyork and her friends solved some important crimes today. She caught a thief who had been selling and then stealing-back pet empaths known as owsers."*

Rebecca smiled. She was sitting on one of the lift-up pillows in Ms. Vis's front room. Next to her sat Iris and Iri. Watson stood by the doorway and beamed.

Ms. Vis continued to read: *"Aided by Mrs. Jay Gregory Van Stebbins (lineage traced to Mayflower, below); the faithful Watson, a robot series #1960gh483406745 (see circuitry below); and two friends, Iris and Iri of the Rainbow Galaxy (father and mother's color lines below), young Ms. Jasons trapped the infamous Gray Man from Chameleon III (see previous arrest record below) in his disguise as, variously, a Pettery owner, a mop, a tree, a fog, a newspaper, and a fire hydrant."*

Ms. Vis finished reading the article, which went on to describe the entire day-long search.

"And now," said Ms. Vis, "I have a sur-prise." She handed around a plate of soy-cakes and berryjuice. "I have bought the remains of the dreadful gray man's Pettery. I am going to give a pet to each of the fifty-five other people who lost an owser. And I want to give each of you, my new friends, a pet, too."

She went into her second room and came back with an enormous box. She set it down on the floor. Strange sounds were coming from the box.

"Iris and Iri, these are for you," said Ms. Vis. She reached into the box and pulled out two very rare ribbon snakes. There was an orange-striped one for Iris, a blue-striped one for Iri. The ribbon snakes wound themselves around the Rainbow kids' fingers. Iris put hers in her hair where it knotted itself into a bow. Iri used his as a tie.

"And Watty, this is for you," said Ms. Vis. She handed him a bottle of slate-colored marbeliters, little round animals that looked just like ball bearings. "They need only a quart of oil once a month and live pretty nearly forever."

Watson took the bottle and gazed at it

for the longest time. Then his face plate turned a pale pink.

"And last, but certainly not least, Rebecca," said Ms. Vis. "With my warmest thanks." She took a furry muffle from the box and put it over Rebecca's shoulder. The muffle fell asleep right away. "To remind you of the first time we saw the gray man—as a mop."

"Thank you, Ms. Vis," said Rebecca. "But if you won't be hurt, I would like to give my muffle to my brother Adam. He's much better at caring for things than I am."

Ms. Vis shook her head. "But my dear, how can I reward you?"

"All I'd like is to get to take your owser for a walk every once in a while. Because . . . because—"

Ms. Vis nodded. "I understand completely, my dear. Because of the way the owser makes you feel. I wish I could share my owser with all the other people who lost their owsers. Of course. Every Tuesday at three o'clock, my autocycle will come and pick you up. Then you may come here and walk the owser. Only you must promise me one thing."

Rebecca looked up, her face flushed and happy. "Anything," she said.

"You must never tie my owser to a hydrant."

Rebecca laughed out loud. "Not ever. Not to a gray hydrant—or a red one either. Just in case."

Jane Yolen, well-known for her fairy tales, science fiction, and fantasy stories, is the author of over fifty books for children, including *The Robot and Rebecca: The Mystery of the Code-Carrying Kids* and *The Boy Who Spoke Chimp,* both Knopf Capers books. A lecturer and critic, Ms. Yolen's articles and stories have appeared in *The New York Times, Cricket, Horn Book, Language Arts, Childhood Education* and *Fantasy & Science Fiction.*

Ms. Yolen received a B.A. from Smith College and an M.Ed. from the University of Massachusetts. She has been a recipient of the Christopher Medal, the Golden Kite Award, and a National Book Award nomination.

Ms. Yolen lives in a farmhouse in Hatfield, Massachusetts with her family.

Other Capers books by Knopf:

"I hope the Capers signal a return to the important role light, easy-to-read fiction has in getting children into the reading habit."

—DONALD J. BISSETT,
Children's Literature Center,
Wayne State University